AF449849

UNLEASH YOU

10 steps to unleash your true potential and live a fulfilling life

INSPIRING JATIN

Clever Fox
PUBLISHING

Chennai • Bangalore

CLEVER FOX PUBLISHING
Chennai, India

Published by CLEVER FOX PUBLISHING 2022
Copyright © Inspiring Jatin 2022

All Rights Reserved.
ISBN: 978-93-56481-17-6

This book has been published with all reasonable efforts taken to make the material error-free after the consent of the author. No part of this book shall be used, reproduced in any manner whatsoever without written permission from the author, except in the case of brief quotations embodied in critical articles and reviews.

The Author of this book is solely responsible and liable for its content including but not limited to the views, representations, descriptions, statements, information, opinions and references ["Content"]. The Content of this book shall not constitute or be construed or deemed to reflect the opinion or expression of the Publisher or Editor. Neither the Publisher nor Editor endorse or approve the Content of this book or guarantee the reliability, accuracy or completeness of the Content published herein and do not make any representations or warranties of any kind, express or implied, including but not limited to the implied warranties of merchantability, fitness for a particular purpose. The Publisher and Editor shall not be liable whatsoever for any errors, omissions, whether such errors or omissions result from negligence, accident, or any other cause or claims for loss or damages of any kind, including without limitation, indirect or consequential loss or damage arising out of use, inability to use, or about the reliability, accuracy or sufficiency of the information contained in this book.

About the Author

Jatin Gupta popularly known as Inspiring Jatin is an Award-winning Life Coach, Healer, Guinness World Records Winning Participant, TEDx Speaker, Multiple times International Bestselling Author, India's First Non-Fiction Book Writing Coach, and a Motivational Speaker. He is also a Skill India Trainer certified by MEPSC, the Government of India. Google features his brand in *Best Life Coach in India* category. Inspiring Jatin is the awardee of the *45 under 45 edition* amongst the brightest young minds from across the nation belonging to different industry sectors.

For many years, Jatin lived an incomplete and unfulfilled life. His hard work, resilience, enthusiasm, and conviction brought him a long way. However, his past and limiting beliefs blocked his growth in various areas of life. His self-experience and observations of the depth of pain and problems people go through in their daily lives motivated him to contribute to many lives as **Inspiring Jatin.**

Now, he works with young folks who may be unaware of their vision in life, are not enjoying their current work/ business, and are struggling to overcome negative emotions from the past, that is holding them back from success. Such people find themselves unable to make the right decisions and are struggling with marriage and love relationships.

In his journey of transforming lives, Jatin has touched over 20,000+ lives with his coaching and speaking events and helped break through the obstacles that were holding them back in life. After having touched so many lives with his coaching sessions and earning the title of Inspiring Jatin, his **mission** is to impact more than one million lives in the next five years. His **vision** is to equip as many lives as possible with the tools and techniques to exert the power of choice over whatever life may throw at them.

He also believes that non-fiction books can evoke transformation. Hence, he is on another mission of helping non-fiction writers become published authors and contribute to people's lives.

ABOUT THE AUTHOR

He loves to dance, listen to music, travel, and spend time with his family. The purpose of his life is to impact many more lives and be known for his work.

Let's Follow him on Social Media:

www.inspiringjatin.com

Contents

Foreward

I'll bet that there's one excuse you have in your life that is keeping you away from executing specific actions. They may go from specific reasons like 'I'm timid so can't get any place in life' to essential reasons like 'incredible things don't occur to people like me'.

Either way, these reasons are superfluous and unnecessary. Incidentally it's not even that we bear excuses which prevent us from getting somewhere, it's simply the way that our goals are close to nothing, and they don't test our cutoff points.

Try not to start satisfying your potential tomorrow, do it now, regardless of whether it implies you're reducing your mid-day break. Truly set these means in motion and start being the individual you wish to be, the individual you're intended to be.

1. The Benefits to Unleashing Your True Potential

Synopsys

Floating through life on the casual mentality doesn't permit a person to get doubt free potential out of life. At some point individuals don't understand there is something else entirely to life than their little universes. In the journey to discovering what is out there, the initial one ought to figure out how to release the likely powers from the inside. When you have found the love of your life, you feel like everything is perfect, right? That is how magical love is. It can turn a grey world into a colourful one, a frown into a smile and melt frozen cold hearts.

The Benefits

Having the option to rest soundly consistently is only one of the advantages of arriving at one's actual potential. At the point when the psyche is open and free there are no limitations to its quiet solace, subsequently the capacity to rest soundly.

Floating during a time without feeling the pressure and stresses every other person appears to have in their lives is additionally an advantage to releasing one's latent capacity.

Having a steady mentality of harmony, assists with welcoming on the experience of genuine joy and happiness. Achieving this degree of harmony in the lone manner completes one's life.

Releasing the genuine potential additionally permits an individual to find a sense of contentment from the inside. This at that point shields the psyche from managing the intensity and pessimism in the workplace. This likewise guarantees the individual doesn't turn to utilizing such antagonism themselves.

The energy to interface with affection ones is upgraded, when one has serenely achieved the genuine potential throughout everyday life.

There could be no further need to pursue things that have minimal enduring worth. Time invested with family is energy all around spent.

Being agreeable in the organization of individuals from varying backgrounds and all extraordinary ethnic foundations unmistakably shows the accomplishment to the genuine potential in a person.

The vast majority will in general adhere to the things they are OK with and stay away from anything new, however an individual who has figured out how to will arrive at their expected lives by an alternate outlook out and out.

2. Decide What Areas of Your Life Need Change

Synopsis

Making decisions to embark on something new is quite scary. Furthermore, if it involves something totally new and foreign the level of fear is further enhanced. There are usually many factors to deal with and this will put further pressure on the decision to change. Healthy Relationship

Choose

Adding to this, settling on a choice to change doesn't generally happen when the positive components in the circumstance dwarf the negative. Consequently, the typical situation is to remain in the trench and proceed with the current circumstance.

Anyway, when the case is the inverse, where the current circumstance's negative components dwarf the positive, and afterwards, something should be done to improve the chances of acquiring achievement.

One approach to urge the person to make the main significant stride is to venture back and view the circumstance as dispassionately as could be expected. Settling on a firm choice to roll out an improvement is vital.

Choosing what changes should have been made would empower the circumstance to begin turning itself around. Other than these basic advances, every individual should gauge the chances of accomplishment while believing the progressions to be made.

Have a "working paper" done on the apparent changes and their functions to accomplish these potential changes. This will give the outlook a clearer image of the necessities required to roll out the improvement.

After taking a gander at a circumstance or issue dispassionately, the cycle to change can begin to happen. The most widely recognized things that the vast majority consider changing are their professions.

Not many individuals are genuinely happy with their present circumstance and consistently see something better accessible.

Another zone that the vast majority try to improve in will be in their connections. As these progressions most occasions need to go through upsetting stages before the quiet is acquired, there is generally a ton of dread in settling on the choice, as it is undoubtedly huge.

3. Channel Positive Energy into Your Life

Synopsis

It is a prevalent view both in the logical and non-logical world that everything is associate with and by energy. There is sufficient energy, and there is terrible energy, as everything is energy. Understanding Problems.

Utilizing this premise of point of view, the end that everything individual encounters comprise either sure energy or negative energy, which in some relating way is directed by the activities in a specific circumstance.

Favorable Influence

To be the recipient of just tremendous and positive energy, an individual should know its association and compare responses constantly.

An exceptionally incredible line of reasoning to consider is, we show into reality our opinion and feel firm about it.

Logical examinations have demonstrated that musings and sentiments are unadulterated energy elements. Accordingly, these energy substances, be it sure or negative, is the thing that directs the result of the point of view and relating activity.

Put, think positive get positive, and think negative get negative. There are a few time-tested techniques that are prescribed to channel positive energy into one's life. Here is a portion of those proposals:

Control the measures of media presented to the person. Being continually besieged with negative pictures and noisy forceful music doesn't make a positive and quiet mentality.

Build up a decent attestation framework and continually rehash the confirmation yet with complete conviction. This will permit the inner mind to become acclimated to it and begin to embrace it as a situation.

Be careful about individuals and conditions encompassing the person. The positive leaning individuals surrounding the individual won't just make a positive attitude by transmitting positive energy continually. This energy can be firmly felt and is infectious in a suitable manner.

4. How Important Is Goal Setting

Synopsis

Getting the best out of life often requires a lot of focus and hard work. Without these two elements it can prove to be an uphill task or even impossible. Almost nothing comes at the drop of a hat. However, there are some methods that can prove to be quite useful along the way. Having a plan in place before embarking on the journey is definitely a good idea.

Goals

This process is called goal setting. This is one way to achieve what is needed to reach the goal within a specific time frame and to the satisfaction of all concerned. Most successful completion of projects has this one thing in common – goal setting.

The elements involved in goal setting are relatively simple and should be so. Setting complicated and unreasonable steps to reaching the goal is foolish. It can harm the results.

Some things to include when setting a goal are as follows:

- Charting out a long-term plan

- Mapped out the time frame for each progressive step

- Tasks and deadline in specifics

- Personnel involved in the execution of the plan

This is one of the best ways to keep track of what is happening and how well the exercise is going. Goal setting is critical for other reasons, too, like giving everyone involved a vision to work towards and a sense of accomplishment after each step is successfully achieved.

Besides this, goal setting is also beneficial because it can also bring to attention any weak points that need to be addressed immediately before the project takes a wrong turn or churns the incorrect results. It can also function as a benchmark to gauge any further needs that could prove helpful to the task at hand or any future endeavours.

5. How to Set Goals Correctly

Synopsis

Everyone should have goals in life, and most people do. However, when planning for these goals, there are many varied tried and trusted methods to choose from.

Having some knowledge of the various recommendations will help anyone work out their goal plan. Being as well informed as possible allows the individual to avoid setting the goals so high that it would be impossible to reach and eventually cause failure.

Do It Correctly

Being specific when setting goals is a very important point to adhere to. When there is no specific outline, the tendency to be vague is ever-present, which can work against the goal as the mind cannot focus on the clear picture of what is wanted and needed.

This vagueness also gives too much "freedom", and because there are not many restrictions, mistakes are inevitable and very likely.

Having a measurable way to determine the progress of the goal is another way to ensure completion and success. Every goal must have a time frame that is measured against tangible materials. The progress made must match the time frame and the expected results based on the said time frame. This check and balance method ensure the necessary adjustments are made immediately upon discovery and not only when the progress had encountered problems.

Achievable goal scenarios are something that should be carefully considered before mapping out the method to achieve the goal is done. The feeling of excitement and zest to complete the project will quickly wane once the realization dawns that the goal is unachievable.

Perhaps seeking opinions of those around who know the capabilities of the individual is an indication of sorts as to whether the goal will succeed.

Besides being a gauging tool for reaching the goal, timelines are also wise because this ensures the completion date target is met.

If there is no timeline in place, then there is no sense of urgency and no discipline.

6. Define Who You Look Up to And Emulate Them

Synopsis

One of the worst relationship killers is no other than your own mind. The moment you start thinking negatively without any basis, that is the time when your relationship will come crashing down. If you are the kind of person who thinks negatively towards the people around you and towards your partner, it is you who has a problem; not them.

People Who Know- How

Today, many people idolize others because they like what they see and because they want to be the person they worship. The same concept can be applied to the individual looking to set a goal.

Defining the specific points that draw the individual to be attracted to the person they are trying to emulate is exciting and enlightening.

Often this requires an in-depth study of the idol or object of idolization itself.

Listing all the admired points of the person or object idolized and slowly incorporating these points into one's own life allows the person to grow more confident in themselves and even cause an improvement in their lives along the way.

As each point is successfully met or achieved, the individual's confidence level becomes more apparent, which further gives the individual the much-needed boost to strive for even bigger things.

In defining and emulating someone, the individual also gets to physically see the "end product" to find such strong admiration.

This is beneficial if the qualities sought are positive. Thus, by emulating the positive qualities, the person's life circumstances benefit.

Caution should be exercised when making this choice as it will impact the success of the goal and the processes required to reach it. Even if the goal has finally reached these qualities used in the emulation process may have become such an integral part of the individual that it further benefits other aspects of the individual's life.

7. Draw Good Karma by Always Being Grateful

Synopsis

Breezing through life is a beautiful way to life. Everything comes so quickly, and the circumstances are always wonderfully bearable. This scenario is rare indeed, in today's world of mainly worry and stress, but a wonderful thing to be able to attain.

Pull In Good

The popular thought is, do good – get good, does perhaps ring true to some extent. Kindness and gratitude are virtues that can be cultivated and strengthened. Still, it would be prudent to practice both these virtues together. Both these elements need to be entwined for them to come across as genuine.

Doing things to benefit someone else helps to promote the virtue of kindness, allowing the individual to experience inner peace and joy.

However, the exercise must be genuine on this excellent by-product to manifest itself. When an act of kindness has been extended, the feeling of gratefulness from the recipient is tremendous, especially if the action itself was timely and much needed.

Besides being beneficial to the recipient of the kind act, good karma can also be derived for the recipient who learns how to be grateful for the front of kindness received. When one is in a state of gratefulness, the body and mind undergo a specific change, which softens the heart. The humbling effect it has genuinely allows the individual to appreciate things more and be more in tune with surrounding elements.

Those who have been on both sides of the coin realize that gratitude is the cornerstone for the law of attraction. In learning how to be grateful for everything one has, the good karma that is drawn from this attitude is not only phenomenal; it is also genuine.

8. Why It Is Important to Keep Learning

Synopsis

Constantly being eager to learn things no matter at what age is not only beneficial in terms of knowledge but also helps to keep the mind and body alert.

Keeping abreast with the latest information of various kinds allows the individual to be well informed and generally knowledgeable in almost any topic or fields.

Keep Growing

Most people associate learning with education, and this is not entirely correct. Being willing to be exposed and informed to anything, anytime and anywhere, is a form of the learning process. The process of learning is ever-present in an individual's life, from learning a new skill to handling family issues. Even taking up a new hobby is learning or acquiring a new skill.

People who are keen to try new things and at the same time pick up a few beneficial tips along the way are people who have come to realize the importance of growing from strength to strength in life. By remaining stubbornly in the mindset that one does not need to learn new things as age progresses is indeed a vast folly for the individual concerned and those around him or her.

Even if the new information learnt does not bring about an immediate benefit or use, it does not mean the whole exercise of acquiring this further information is useless. It is not unusual for the learnt matter to come in handy at some later stage.

There are benefits like saving money because the information learnt may help resolve a problem without hiring or paying for outside help. In tackling the problem and deriving successful results, the individual also benefits mentally because of the satisfaction generated from independence.

Being willing to learn new things or pick up new skills constantly shows the individual's willingness to grow. It allows for the opportunities to present themselves. Because of this good trait, the individual will notice a vast area of options always available.

9. Don't Be Afraid of Change

Synopsis

Being afraid of change is a common and normal experience most people go through at one point or another in their lives. Growing comfortable or having already reached their "comfort zone" in life often makes people extremely wary of the prospect of change.

The results of which is strong resistance to any change at all. However, it would benefit all to embrace the prospect of change with an open mind and a positive attitude.

Alter Things

Some of the issues one may have to deal with when attempting or before considering the change are fear of the unknown, doubt in oneself, isolation, and agonizing over decisions, forgetting to consider other options, focusing too much on the external picture and limiting the resources.

All these issues can hold an individual in the grip of fear to make the change.

Fear of the unknown can be paralyzing indeed. The human mind is more than capable of conjuring up images of every possible adverse scenario that could materialize if the change is attempted, thus effectively sabotaging any positive steps taken to make the change.

However, if the human mind can do this, it would make sense to correctly assume that the human mind is also capable of conjuring equally positive images to bring about the zest and confidence to step up and make the change desired.

Another fear to overcome would doubt oneself and capabilities. Most people tend to sell themselves short simply because they are unwilling to step out of their comfort zones and try something totally new.

The correct attitude should be open-mindedness, and by having this, the fear of failing becomes less of the focal point. Instead, the person can accept that they did try something new at the very worst, although it failed, and there are no "what if" nagging thoughts.

10. The Downside of Not Being Where You Should Be

Synopsis

Many people never reach their true potential because of their fear of failure. They would rather stay in their comfort zone and dream of things that could be rather than taking steps to make it happen.

For some, this is a situation they can accept and live with comfortably. In contrast, for others, this discontent can cause severe mental and physical health issues.

Alter Things

One of the downsides of not being where one should be is that there is a constant discontentment in the individual's life.

This discontentment can and will lead to problems in other areas of the individual life, from health to wealth.

When it comes to the work environment, the discontent here can result in losing interest in the task at hand or not putting in the best efforts to ensure a good job is done. When this happens, the negative repercussions can cause the individual to lose the already tenuous standing in the work environment and further dampening any chances of moving upwards, career-wise.

One's full potential cannot be reached if the current position in life does not match the perceived capabilities of the individual. This is also another consequence of not being where one should be. Calculated risk is never taken; thus, potentials are never explored nor reached. This scenario also does not allow the individual to remember that other options may be available due to taking the extra step.

"Tying" oneself down because of the current perks enjoyed contributes to the failure to reach one's potential in life. This is usually when the fear of the unknown is prevalent in stopping the individual from taking the risk to step out of the comfort zone. Fear of losing whatever is already available against whatever could be gained is the downside of not being where one should and can be.

Wrapping Up

It amazes me how many individuals I know have ambitions for where they would like to go in the future yet have no real plan on how they would like to arrive there.

Rather plainly, you're never going to reach your full potential if you carry on with the precise same lifestyle that you are living nowadays. I'm sorry, but someplace along the line, things will have to switch, and you might need to compromise.

About Life Coaching

Over last few years, Coaching has become one of the best ways to create positive changes and lasting results in life.

A Life Coach:

- Helps you discover 'Who You Are'

- Makes you to identify 'What Motivates & Drives you'

- Works with you to 'Eradicate your Limiting Beliefs'

- Helps you to get clarity about 'What you want in Life'

- Guides you to 'Set Goals' with a step-by-step process to achieve them

- Enables you to 'Make Empowering Decisions' in life

- Makes You 'More Responsible for Your Actions and Commitments'

- Helps you to 'Tap into your Blind Spots and Grow as a Person'

If you or someone known to you feels the need for life coaching, I can be reached on WhatsApp at +918826268998

www.inspiringjatin.com

Voice of Clients

Source- Google Page: https://g.page/inspiringjatin?gm

- ❖ Inspiring Jatin is a magician who helped me love myself like I never did and explore the potential I never knew about myself. Thank you so much sir for transforming my life and helping me find the purpose of my life. I highly recommend his coaching for becoming a Happier and Successful version of yourself.

- ❖ Jatin has just in one session helped me understand what has been bringing me down and stopping me from achieving the one thing that I want in life. He's helped me delve deeper into surface level issues such as low levels of self confidence and assertiveness to a deeper desire for financial freedom. He's helped me understand how this one desire or the fact that it's not yet achieved has affected my overall personality and behaviour. He has also helped me understand what are the negative patterns in my life and that to achieve what I want I will have to take action and actively work towards breaking them down.

❖ I wish I would have met you years ago and saved my years that I wasted in Anxiety and Overthinking. After your coaching sessions, I found myself and know what I want in my life. Thank you Jatin sir for being Truly Inspiring and helping me change my life for good. Highly Highly Recommended for finding help for any life related issue.

❖ He is a man who knows how to get you out of low state and bring the best out of you. Thank you Inspiring Jatin for your incredible coaching.

❖ Jatin is Incredibly good with what he does! Glad to have known him and worked with him! I highly recommend his Life Coaching Venture! And excited to get hands on his upcoming book!

❖ I have found Jatin to be an exceptionally intelligent person. He has learned a lot from his own life experiences, and weaves this knowledge into understanding his clients. His coaching is, hence, powerful and effective, as he connects with the emotions of the clients and plans his strategy to help them, accordingly. This brings the desired transformation. I wish him great success and power to help as many as possible.

- ❖ Inspiring Jatin is one of the best Life Coaches in Delhi NCR and India. His Life Coaching sessions will help you to gain. Guys, please join him to change ur life.

- ❖ Jatin is Great motivator, Enthusiastic and Diligent, He always inspires to perform better and He is Master in his art to get best out of you.

- ❖ I have had a wonderful experience of the discovery session with Jatin. It was very comfortable to share the truths about myself my fears my obstacles my dreams with him, which i myself was hiding away from since long. He explained very explicitly the importance of knowing our own self and working for your gaols after beating the obstacles. As per Jatin, this may be done by the 10-week program offered by him as a coach, but ultimately you have to take your own actions. It was overall very good experience with Jatin.

- ❖ Jatin is a very professional and thorough coach, someone who wants to make a difference in people's life. Highly recommended.

.... and many more.

Book your Free Strategy Call NOW!
https://click.inspiringjatin.com/stgycall

Acknowledgments

Firstly, I would like to thank God for giving me the best parents, powerful mentors, and child that anyone can ever dream of.

Secondly, a big hug to the man who always showers his blessings on me from heaven and is still around to protect me- my father, Late Mr Suresh Gupta. He was so humble, gentle, loving, and caring caring. He loved me more than he loved himself, and my mother echoes this. He left me too early; however, I am glad I picked the quality of being a loving father from him.

Thirdly, to the woman who has gone through so much in life that her story can inspire the whole world, my mother, Ms Rani Gupta. During most of her life, she worked very hard to raise me so beautifully and fulfil all my unrealistic demands, even during the tough times. Her dream of giving excellent education to me and inspiring the whole world kept me pepped up to live her dreams. Her attitude of never giving up and taking actions to move ahead in life made me tolerant and resilient.

Her struggle of raising me despite hiccups in life and always encouraging me to value my essence is a true reflection of who I am today. Thank you, Mom!

A big thanks to my son, Master Girik J Gupta, for being one of the most significant buzz moments (when you feel out of the world) of my life. Without him, I would have settled with my life at the ordinary and wouldn't have dared to dream big. He is an electric current of the bulb inside me. Girik, you were, you are and will always be the only love of my life. Thank you for being my son.

A big bouquet of gratitude to my mentors Arfeen Khan, Sorav Jain, Rishi Jain, & Mitesh Khatri for making my journey of Entrepreneurship smooth and easy.

Special thanks to the multi talented wonder girl who came into my life out of nowhere and earned an indispensable space in my life. Most of the moments spent with her turned out to be my buzz moments and will continue to be. Her life journey, warrior spirit, multiple modalities, and happy go lucky attitude incited me in many ways.

Thank you, DD (Divyadeep), for offering your unfiltered and selfless friendship that I would like to cherish till my last breath.

Last, however, not least, I want to thank **YOU** for picking this book and taking ownership to Unleash Yourself. After reading this book, I am sure you will gain clarity of ***What to Achieve***, ***When to Achieve*** and ***How to Achieve***.

Do not forget to write to me about how this book helped you. Please do leave your feedback on Amazon. It will encourage many people like you to buy this book and inspire them to take responsibility to make their life happy & content.

Love you all,

Inspiring Jatin

www.inspiringjatin.com

author@inspiringjatin.com

Praise For Author

Book: BREAKFREE TO BREAKTHROUGH

"I love the way you have authored Kabir's character in your manuscript. Your book is a great inspiration for the youth to accept if they are not living a happy life and seek professional help from a life coach."

Paras Chhabra: *Indian Model, Actor, Splitsvilla 5 Winner & Bigg Boss 13 Finalist*

Books By This Author

BREAK FREE TO BREAK THROUGH: Shit Happens In Life; Your Happiness Is Your Responsibility

Everyone will find their story in this book and remind them that shit happens in life, and that this is just the pattern life follows. Even if they don't find their story in this book, they might be able to relate to some of the incidents from their life that are holding them back.

The book shall guide them on releasing any pain, guilt, or discomfort they might be carrying from their childhood. It will nudge them to take responsibility for overcoming their limiting beliefs; to evoke self-belief and achieve massive success in all areas of life.

For Parents, To-be Parents, Guardians, Teachers, this book should act as an alert manual for them and awaken the much-needed consciousness in their respective role. It shall navigate them on how to help raise happy human beings, loving spouses, and conscious parents, which is way beyond the cliché of scoring high in academic subjects.

Buy it now on Amazon

RESCUE YOUR ROMANCE: The Simplest Secrets to Master Your Love Life

Do you feel guilty because you are the one who made a mistake, or do you find it hard to forgive your partner because of their mistakes? Is your relationship currently hanging by a cliff? Do you want to hold on to it? Well, as long as the waters cover the sea and as the sun rises in the east and sets in the west, it is not too late! You can piece things back together and keep the relationship with the one you love.

Regardless of how stubborn the opposition, nevertheless how far this individual might be from you, nonetheless, how hopeless your state of affairs seems! You need to have a good Relationship Rescue Plan that will help you save your love life.

This book will guide you through the tried and true, proven techniques that you can learn and apply immediately to better your love relationship and even your marriage!

Buy it now on Amazon

THE 10 KEYS TO HAPPINESS: Warning: It Covers Everything You Need to Know About HAPPINESS

Are you happy? Maybe you think you are happy enough? Maybe you have been unhappy for a long time; it seems to be just a part of life. Happiness is the basic foundation that affects the quality of your life. When it comes to happiness, it is important to sit in the driver's seat.

We have all experienced things we don't need in life. However, you can choose to live a painful life or be happy. You are the only one who controls it.

Research shows that happy people tend to do better in all aspects of life. They fall sick less often. They tend to have fewer problems with children or divorce.

Now, you can change your life and give yourself happiness. It doesn't matter where you live, how much money you make, or how old you are. It is never too late to feel happy and truly enjoy life.

These **10 Secrets of Happiness** will help you set out to make your dreams a reality!

Buy it now on Amazon

www.ingramcontent.com/pod-product-compliance
Lightning Source LLC
LaVergne TN
LVHW051512170726
843492LV00002B/896